FOL
D0566249

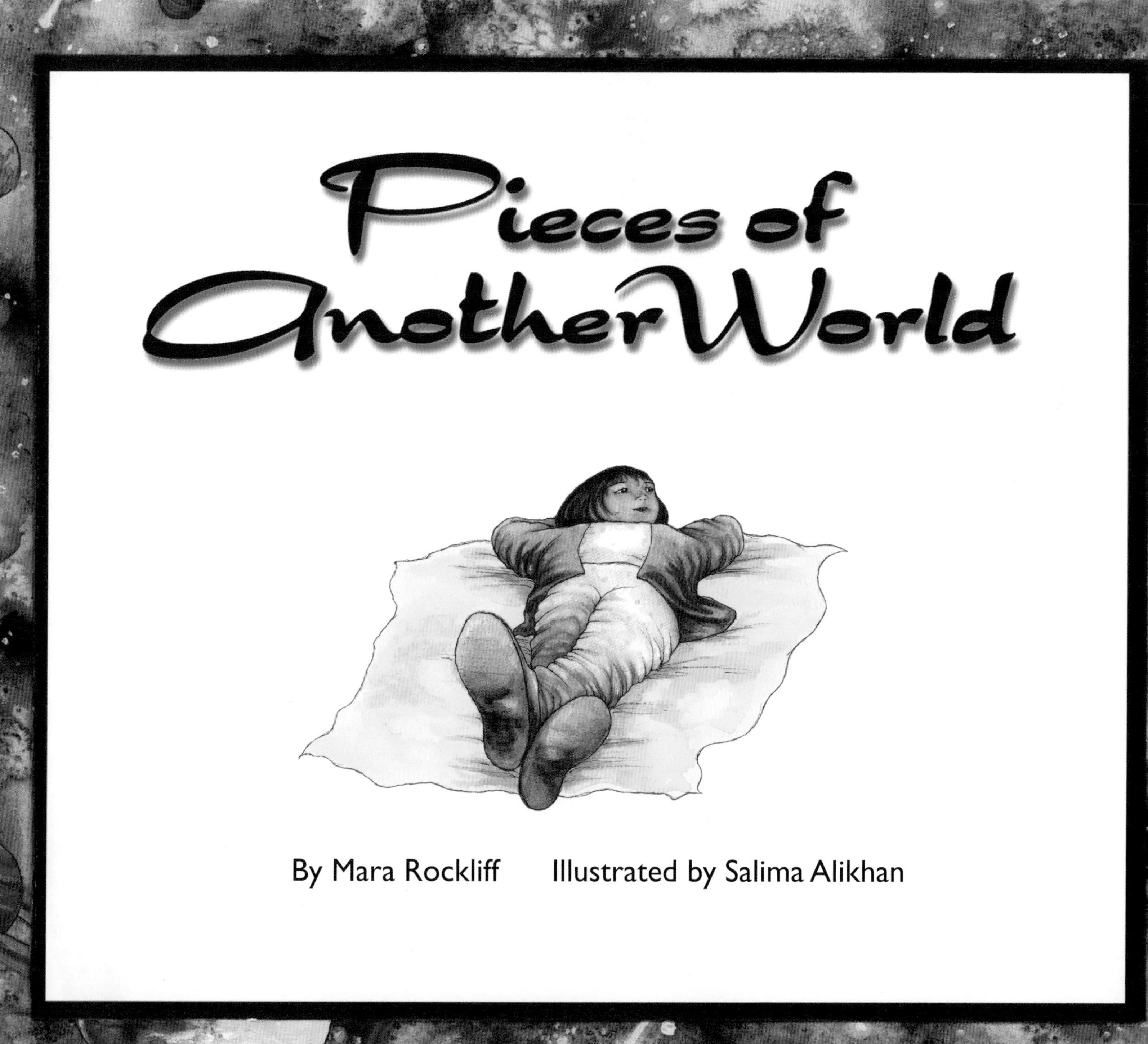

# Pieces of Another World

By Mara Rockliff Illustrated by Salima Alikhan

My ears woke up before the rest of me.

"Jody," whispered Daddy. "Wake up, Jody-bird."

My eyes woke up. But when they opened, it was still dark.

"Is it morning?"

I could hear the smile in Daddy's voice. "Guess it's morning somewhere, but 'round here it's still Saturday night." He tapped me on the head. "Get your shoes on. We're going out."

Now I was awake all over. "Going out? Out where?"

But he was gone.

I pulled my shoes on over my bare feet and clattered into the kitchen.

"Where are we going, Mama?"

She shook her head and put her finger to her lips. She pointed to the door.

I pushed the screen door open. Outside, Daddy sat behind the wheel of our old blue pickup. I climbed in.

"Where are we going, Daddy?"

He flipped on the radio.

"Jody-bird, I've got a sight for you to see."

I bounced in my seat. "What kind of sight?"

"Oh..." He smiled. "Just some pieces of another world."

Then he wouldn't say anything more, just sang along to the music swirling from the radio. *Scoodly oodly bop bop do wada wada...*

I cranked my window down and let the breeze lift up my hair as we rolled through the empty streets. The hardware store was dark, and Carter's drugstore, too.

Out front of the Super Shop, where crowds of cars jostled and nudged all day, a single van sat in the giant parking lot, lonely and lost.

But further on, the Kree-Mee Freeze was lit up like a carnival. Daddy pulled in.

This wasn't the same old daytime Kree-Mee Freeze I knew. No little kids squeezing their cones too hard with ice cream dripping down their hands. No mamas saying *"No you can't have jimmies, now you tell the lady chocolate or vanilla."*

Inside I saw teenagers out on their Saturday night, eating hamburgers and playing pinball. I felt a little funny in my PJs and my shoes. One boy grinned at me and said, "Hey, sleepwalker," but he didn't say it mean so I grinned back.

Daddy got a chocolate cone and I got rainbow jimmies on vanilla. We walked back to the truck, licking our cones.

"I've never been in town so late at night," I said. "It *is* a piece of another world."

Daddy smiled. "Maybe so. But this is not the sight I'm taking you to see."

We drove out of town, past the gas station and past the farm supply and lumber yard. On my tongue, the ice cream melted cold and sweet. The night blew its warm breath across my face, and that was sweet, too.

A big dark something bounded out into the road and Daddy stopped the truck. It was a deer, with antlers like the branches of a tree. It stared at us, wide-eyed, till Daddy flipped the headlights off. When he flipped them on again, the deer was gone.

We came to the big field by the lake. In the morning, it's a swimming lake. In the evening, it's a fishing lake.

But now, there were no kids in swimming suits with tire tubes, no men with fishing rods and sharp hooks hanging from their vests.

Daddy pulled way out into the empty field, and I peered out over the headlights. "Look! There's a cat up on the hill!"

He shook his head. "That's a fox. Red foxes like to spend the night on high ground."

"Why?"

He curled his hands into binoculars around his eyes. "Why do you think?"

"So they can see?"

Daddy nodded. "A fox is curious. It doesn't like to miss a thing. Just like you, Jody-bird."

He cut the engine, and the quiet blackness wrapped around us like a blanket.

"I can't see," I told him.

"Give it time," he said. "Your eyes will get used to the dark."

Way across the field, out where the woods began, there came a high, sad wail.

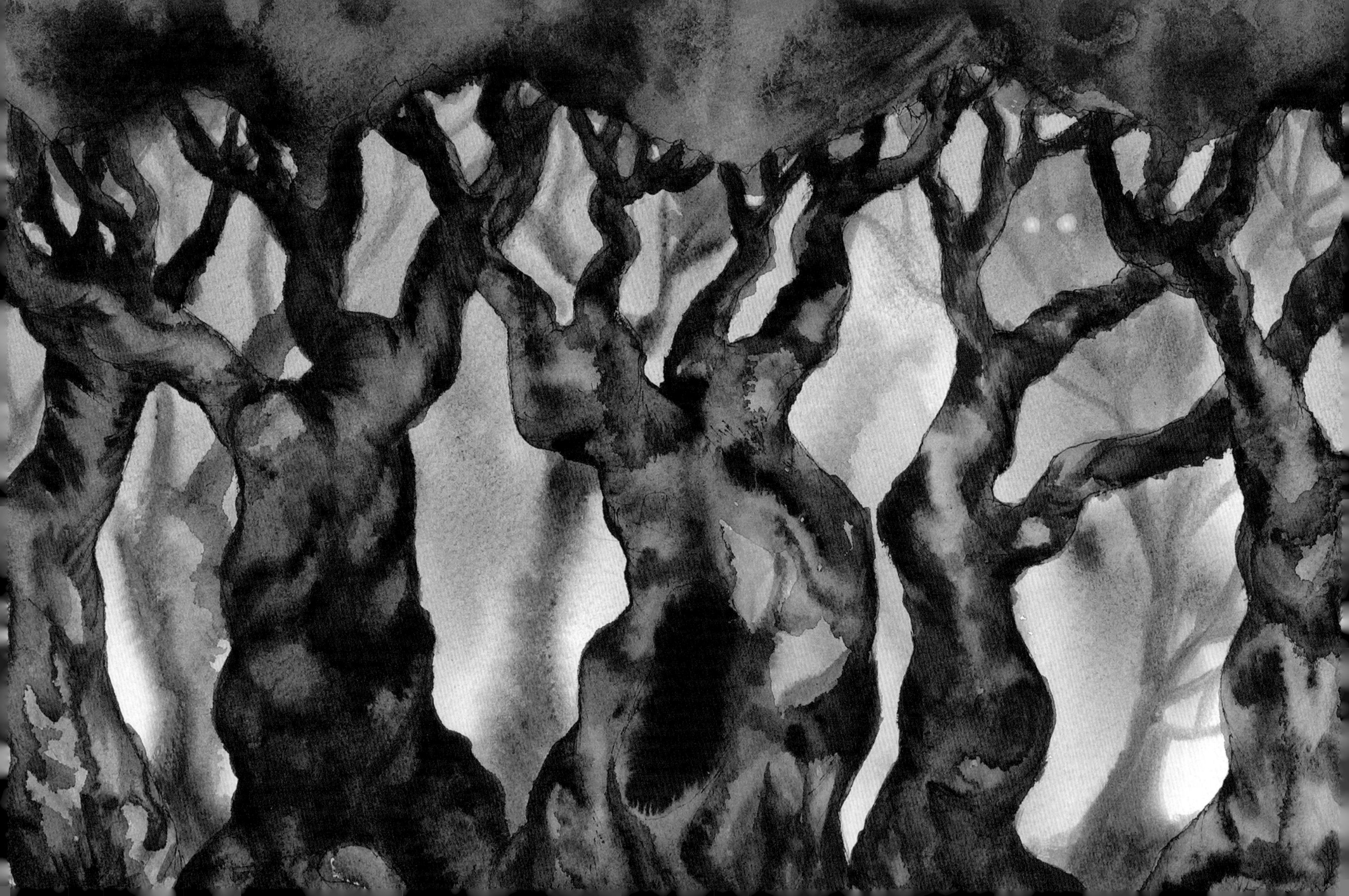

I grabbed his arm. "A baby! Someone left a baby in the woods!"

He said, "It's only a screech-owl."

It sure sounded like a baby crying. I shivered and moved closer to him.

"Listen to this." Daddy leaned out his window and called, *Hoo hoo hoo-hoo!*

From out in the darkness, a call came back. *Hoo hoo hoo-hoo!*

"Who's out there, Daddy?"

"That's another kind of owl," he said. "A barred owl. My daddy used to say it calls, *Who cooks for you?*"

I laughed. And then I said, "You know, I've never been out by the lake so late at night. It *is* a piece of another world."

Daddy smiled. "Maybe so. But that is not the sight I brought you here to see."

By now my eyes could make out shapes and edges in the dark.

He pushed open his door and I pushed open mine. He came around the truck and took my hand to help me down.

I heard the creak and clang as Daddy dropped the tailgate. Then he gave me a boost.

The truck bed felt soft and fuzzy. "You laid blankets out!" I said.

We lay down side by side and stared up at the twinkling sky.

Daddy said, "Watch."

I watched. Nothing happened. Was this all the sight he'd brought me here to see?

Then, suddenly, a streak of white cut through the sky. As soon as I saw it, it was gone.

"What was that?" I asked.

"A meteor. Some folks call it a shooting star."

"Is it a real star?"

Daddy said, "No. Stars are as big as planets—bigger, even. Meteors are tiny, like a pebble or a grain of sand."

"It was high up as an airplane."

"Higher than that," he said. "Much higher."

I frowned. "How can we see something that is so small and so far away?"

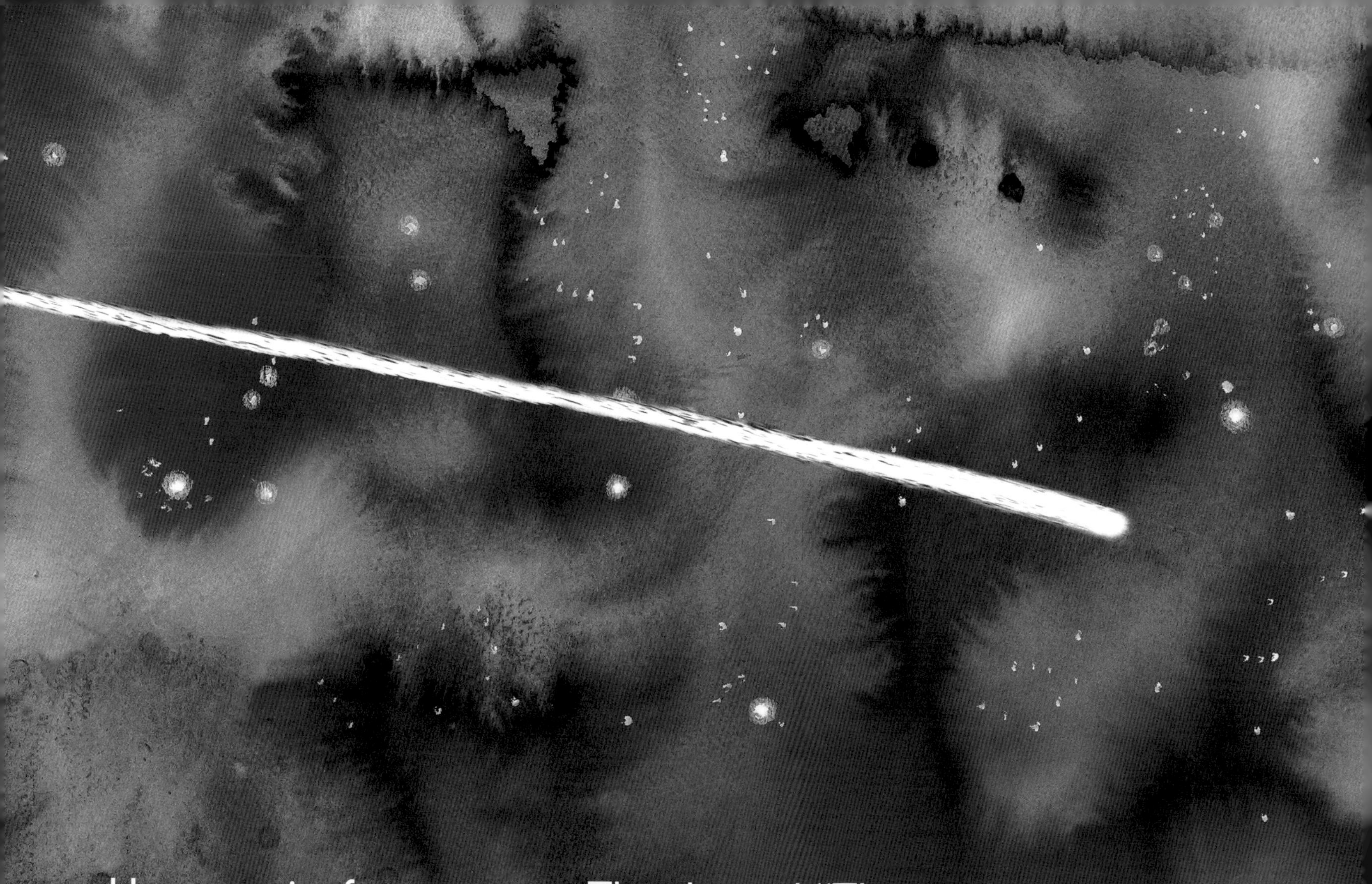

He was quiet for a moment. Then he said, "This truck can go a pretty long way in an hour, can't it?"

"Sure," I said.

"Well, suppose it went that far in just one second."

I laughed. "We'd burn up the road."

"That's what a meteor does," he said. "It slams into our atmosphere and burns right up. We see it burning."

Another white streak shot across the sky.

I said, "I can't believe something so beautiful is just an ordinary pebble."

"It's not ordinary," he said. "Not at all. That pebble is a 'hey-there' from outer space—a tiny piece of some distant world."

I thought about that for a while. And then I smiled.

Daddy and I lay back and watched the meteors together. Most of them were white. A few looked green or yellow. Some even exploded at the end, like fireworks.

But every single one we saw, I whispered the same words:

"Pieces of another world."

## Creative Minds

***Meteor, meteoroid, meteorite—what's the difference?***
A meteoroid is a chunk of rock or metal moving through space. Most are tiny, like a pebble or a grain of sand. But some are as much as a mile wide.
When a meteoroid enters the Earth's atmosphere, it burns up, making a streak of light called a meteor. Sometimes, a large meteoroid does not burn up completely, and it falls to Earth. When it lands, it's called a meteorite.

***Why do meteors shoot by so suddenly?***
Meteoroids move fast! They hit the Earth's atmosphere at up to 150,000 miles per hour. At that speed, it doesn't take long for a speck of space dust to burn up.
To catch sight of a meteor before it's gone, leave your telescope or binoculars at home. The best meteor-spotting tool is a sharp pair of eyes.

***What is a meteor shower?***
Gazing up into the sky on a typical night, you might see one or two meteors in an hour. But during an average meteor shower, you might see a meteor a minute!

***Why all the extra meteors?***
The Earth is passing through a trail of space debris left behind by a comet. A comet is a giant "dirty snowball" orbiting (going around) the sun. As the comet nears the sun, it starts to thaw, letting off a bright tail of gas and bits of dust and rock, which leaves behind a trail. When the Earth's own orbit takes us where the comet has been, we get a meteor shower. (Turn the page to see an illustration.)

### Meteor Math

One of the greatest meteor showers ever was the Leonid storm in 1966, when meteors rained down at a rate of 40 per second.

- If you had been watching, how many would you have seen in 10 seconds?
- How high can you count in 10 seconds? Is that more or less than how many meteors you would have seen?
- How many would you have seen in one minute?
- How many would you have seen in one hour?

## Five Steps to a Fantastic Meteor Watching Party

1. **Plan ahead.** You can see meteors any night, but you'll see most during one of the big yearly meteor showers, such as the Perseids (August) or Leonids (November).

2. **Set your alarm.** The ideal time to spot meteors is in the very early morning—around 4 a.m. If you have a choice, pick a night close to a new moon or when the moon sets before 4 a.m. That will give you better visibility.

3. **Keep it dark.** Get away from street and house lights if you can. If you must use a flashlight, cover the light with red cellophane to keep from spoiling your night vision.

4. **Pack smart.** Bring a blanket, sleeping bag, or folding lawn chair. Dress warmly, even in summer. And don't forget the hot chocolate and Comet Cookies (recipe on next page).

5. **Invite your friends.** Telling jokes and singing songs helps to pass the time between meteors. Or, just lie back quietly and listen to the sounds of the night.

**Look! Up in the sky!** Not every moving object or bright light in the sky is a meteor. Check this list of common night sights:

**Meteors** are bright streaks that shoot by in an instant. Meteors come in many colors: mostly white, but you may also see streaks of yellow, orange-yellow, red, green, blue-green or violet.

**Airplanes** move fast across the sky and have red blinking lights.

**Satellites** move more slowly than meteors and can be seen for several minutes.

**Stars** stay in one place and twinkle.

**Planets** appear to stay in one place, too—unless you watch for weeks!—but they don't twinkle. Look for Mars (red) and Venus (the brightest object in the sky).

Want to learn more about meteors? Go to **www.SylvanDellPublishing.com** and click on ***Pieces of Another World.*** You'll find links to games, puzzles, and information on moon rise/set times and the best nights to see a meteor shower.

## Comet Cookies

Note for classroom teachers: Store-bought chocolate chip cookies will work for this, but try to put some of the "space dust" on top of the cookies.

12-oz. package semi-sweet chocolate chips
12-oz. package miniature chocolate chips
12-oz. package miniature candies, such as M&Ms Mini Baking Bits
18-oz. roll of chocolate chip cookie dough

Mix the chocolate chips and candies in a bowl.
Follow the package directions to prepare the cookies for baking.
Press one tablespoon of candy/chip mix into the top of each cookie.
Bake and cool.

Lay one cookie on a paper plate. The cookie is the comet's head—think of the dough as ice and the candies and chips as bits of "space dust." So what's missing? The tail! You can make a tail with leftover candy/chip mix—about three tablespoons for each comet.

To model a meteor shower, set a lamp in the middle of a table to be the sun. Carefully, "orbit" your comet cookie in an ellipse—long, flat oval—around the lamp. (Watch out for the cord!) As you orbit, shake off bits of candy/chip mix, so that you leave a trail.

Now, set down the plate, then take an orange or small ball—the "Earth"—and roll it slowly around the lamp. A meteor shower results when the Earth passes through the comet's trail.

If you scatter a spoonful of candy/chip mix around the table, you'll see how the Earth crosses paths with a smaller number of meteorites on ordinary nights.

And now, for the final step – eat your comet!

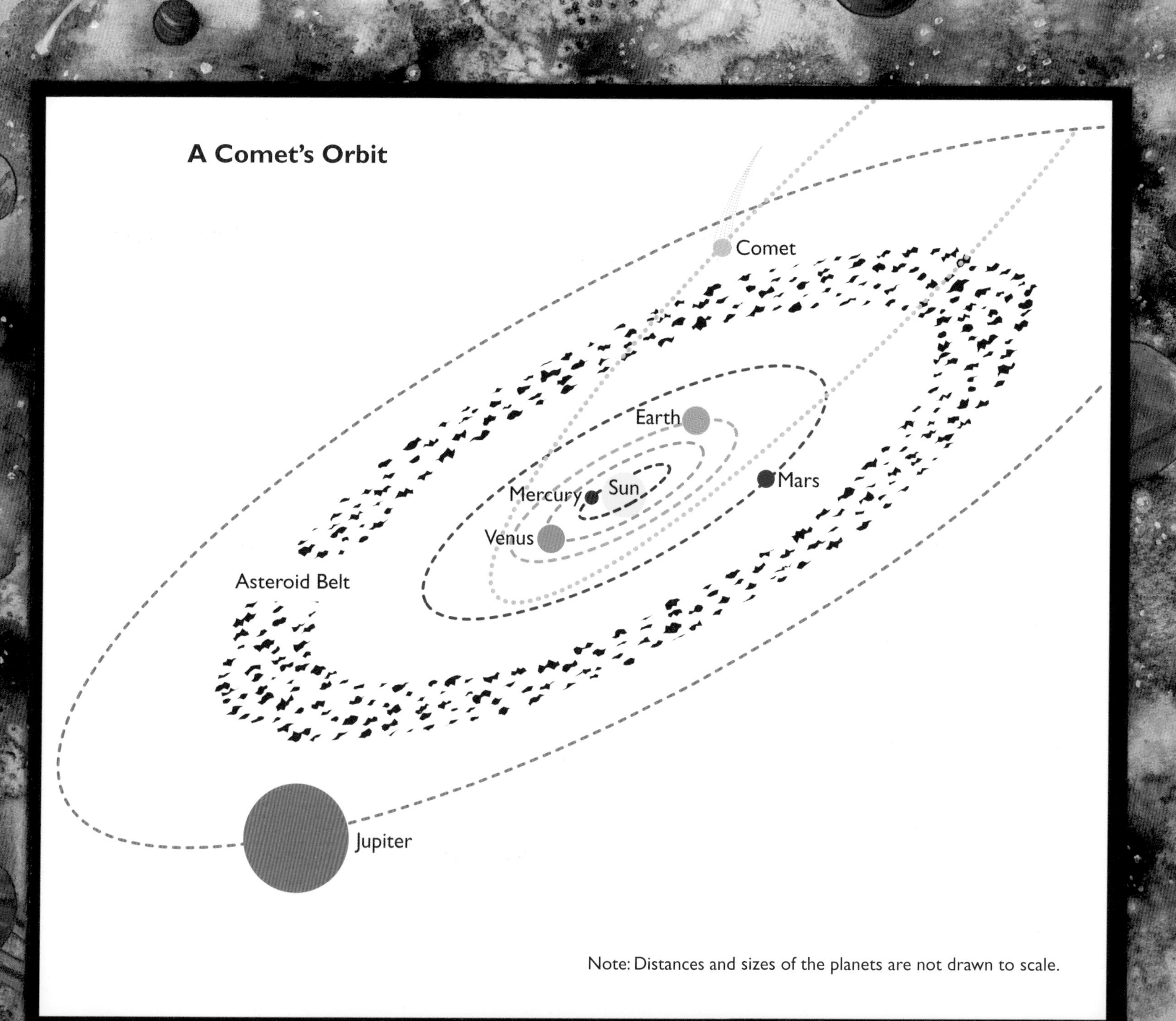
A Comet's Orbit
Comet
Earth
Mars
Mercury
Sun
Venus
Asteroid Belt
Jupiter
Note: Distances and sizes of the planets are not drawn to scale.

Thanks to George Gilba, Senior Technical Specialist at NASA's Goddard Space Flight Center, and Professor Joseph Patterson of the Columbia University Department of Astronomy for reviewing the text for accuracy.

For my parents, who once took us out for ice cream in the middle of the night -- MR
For Mama, Papa, Gobsche, and Shirley -- SA

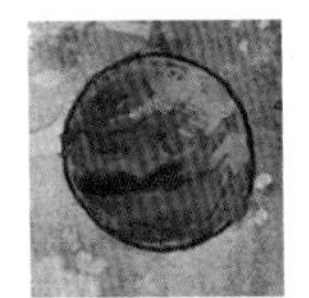

Library of Congress Control Number: 2005921091
A catalog record for this book is available from the Library of Congress.

Summary: A father and child travel through the unfamiliar world of the night to watch a meteor shower.

ISBN: 0-9764943-2-9

Juvenile Fiction: Science & Technology / Astronomy
Juvenile Fiction: Nature & the Natural World
Juvenile Fiction: Family / General

Text Copyright  Mara Rockliff 2005
Illustration Copyright © Salima Alikhan 2005
Craft Illustration Copyrights © Sylvan Dell Publishing 2005
Text Layout and Design by Lisa Downey, studiodowney
Printed in China

All rights reserved. With the exception of the craft section (which may be photocopied by the owner of this book), this book may not be reproduced in any form without permission in writing from the publisher.

Sylvan Dell Publishing
976 Houston Northcutt Blvd., Suite 3
Mt. Pleasant, SC 29464

www.SylvanDellPublishing.com